AF507420

CAR REPAIR
Adventure Of Four Friends

ADVENTURE OF FOUR FRIENDS

Joseph, Ryder, Mary & Jack

Stories

TIME TRAVEL TO FAR FUTURE

Once upon a time, there were four friends Joseph, Mary, Jack and Ryder. One day they stayed together in Jack's house. At that night they watched a movie together.

They all enjoyed the movie, had a good dinner and after some chit chat all went to sleep in the house.

In the night, a thief came into the house quietly. He took the expensive things of the house while all were sleeping. By mistake the thief dropped an expensive glass. There was a huge noise of the glass on the floor – 'Tan Tan Tan....'

Jack woke by hearing the voice of the glass.

He went out of the room and saw that the thief was taking the things. He quickly went to Marry, Ryder and Joseph to wake up them.

Mary asked –"What happened?"

Jack replied–"There seems to be a thief in the house and he is taking the expensive things from here"

"Oh! Lets catch the thief" -said Joseph

Everyone quickly ran towards the thief to get hold of him. Thief ran outside and ran towards a house nearby. He entered into an empty house, the four friends also followed the thief and entered the house.

There was darkness in the house, but some light was coming from the window. After few minutes, they were able to see around in the house in the little light coming from the window.

They saw some instruments and some machines in the house.

This house was actually a laboratory of a scientist named –Dr. Khatra.

In that laboratory scientist Khatra had made a time machine that could took people to the future.

The thief ran fast and was looking for a place to hide him. He entered into the future time machine. Four friends also followed the thief and entered into the machine.

The thief moved backwards as the four friends wanted to get hold of him. As he was moving backwards, he leaned against the wall of the time machine and by mistake the thief pressed a button in the machine, it started the machine with a sound and it started spinning. All of them tried to stop the machine by pressing some random buttons, but it didn't stop. Hearing the noise, scientist also came there and he also tried to stop the time machine but he couldn't stop it.

Mary shouted on the thief – "What have you done, because of you we don't know what is happening and seems the machine is going somewhere". It took off from there and disappeared from

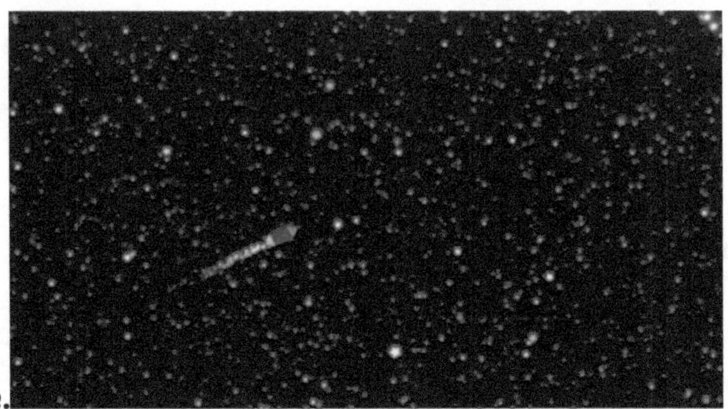

the house.

Machine flew through the universe and after some time the time machine stopped at an unknown place. As they got out of the machine, they were astonished to see the new world!!

They saw a big airplane and a beautiful car. It was a beautiful city.

They realized that they have time traveled into the future.

Joseph said – "Friend see!! There is a big car"

The Thief took advantage of the situation and ran from there. The thief entered into the big car, pressed some buttons and it started flying. Friends saw him-going away from them –flying in the car in the wonder!!

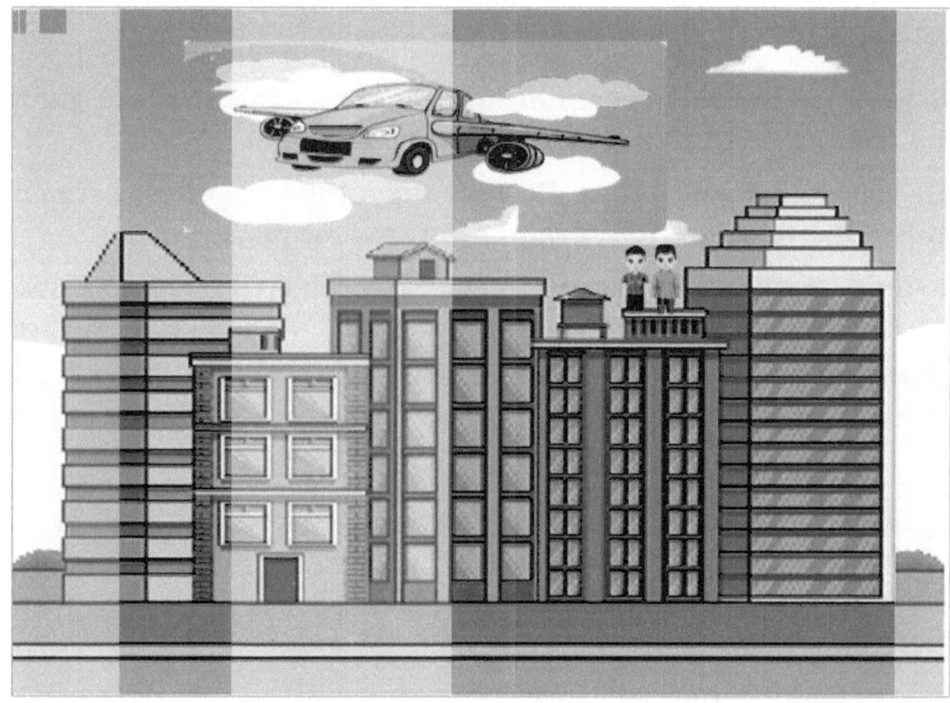

Rider said – 'Wow this is a flying car!!'

Jack – 'Wow, I also want to fly in this car!!"

All were excited to see the flying car.

Rider said – Hey we are in future, we should explore the future and the technology. They realized that time machine had some damage so they thought to first explore the future and then fix the machine, so that they could go back to their homes in their original time.

They roamed here and there and thought for a while, what to do.

Joseph said – "We should ask for help from someone"

Mary said – "It is a good idea"

All agreed and started looking for a person to whom they could ask for help.

They found one gentleman standing nearby and told him their story that they have just landed here and now they want to explore here.

Gentleman looked at them in surprise for a while. He thought a bit and agreed to show them their city.

He was a kind gentleman. He gave them the keys of his car and told them to return it by evening at the same place.

After some hesitation, they thanked him and took his car and started their ride to future

. Four friends first went to the Future museum. Inside it there were very cool bikes that could fly. These bikes were very costly 9999 9999 dollars. There were cool mobiles and robots and the humans could fly using the human Jet flying suit.

They all were surprised to see these things and the Technology.

School was also very good and the students could travel to the Jupiter and even to out of the Milky Way.

Four friends were looking odd as their clothes were not matching to the public.

There were many high sky touching buildings and some buildings were having 500 floors

They thought that they need a place to rest. They were hungry as well. They decided to return to gentleman and return his car.

They reached to gentleman and returned his car and thanked him. Gentleman name was Ronald, he soon became friendly with them.

Gentleman asked them for food at his place.

Four friends agreed and went to his place.

He also helped them with the accommodation at his place.

As the four friends goes into the room they were surprised to see hi-tech room.

Everything was automatic. Machine could cook automatically and when anyone enters the room, TV automatically opens. It was a live 3D on TV.

They all took the bath and sat together.

Joseph said – "We should eat the food and after eating the food we should rest"

They had good dinner with the gentleman.

Ryder said -"I am lucky, I have never eaten such good food"

Joseph and Jack agreed with Ryder.

Jack said tomorrow "We should get ready and should catch the thief. Get him and should return back to our time"

Ronald said –"Let me help you in that".

He dropped them near to the place where they had landed in the future. Their machine was still there, but it was having some issues. Some of the parts were broken.

Ronald said – I know one shop, who can correct this.

As they went to the repairing shop, it couldn't repair the time machine.

They tried with many shops, but no one could correct their time machine because of the parts of The Time Machine were not available. Parts of the Time Machine were very old.

Jack said – "How will we go in the time as the time machine couldn't be repaired"

They thought to try at one more shop. He was an old guy at the shop.

As the old man saw the machine, he was surprised to see the machine and looked to all of them in wonder.

Old man asked them - "From where did you have the machine?"

Mary replied and told the whole story.

Old man laughed – He ha ha..he ha ha.

Ryder asked- Why are you laughing and who are you?

Old Man – kept on laughing and could not control his laughter.

All of them looked at him in surprise.

Old man told them that his name Dr. Tango Khatra and this was the invention of his father Dr. Khatra.

All were shocked and started laughing together.

Old man brought one kit from inside, looked into it and started repairing the machine.

Soon, he was able to fix the machine.

Joseph asked- Oh "We forgot where the thief is."

Dr. Tango Khatra told let me find the thief for you. He brought another instrument from inside the house, it was a tracker.

Old man helped finding the thief with his tracker.

Now they all wanted to return to their time. So they asked every-one to allow them to go back to their time.

Old man said – Wait, take this my invention and give it to my father and tell him that I love him very much. With this the four friends entered into the time machine along with the thief.

They all thanked Dr Khatra, their friend Jacky and said good bye.

Dr. Tango Khatra told them how to go back to their time and helped them started the machine.

After some time they all reached back to their time in Dr. Khatra's home. They all said sorry to Dr. Khatra and told him the entire story. Jack gave Dr.Khatra the invention of his son Dr. Tango Khatra and told him that his son loves him very much.

Dr Kathrin said - "It is ok". He was sentimental to know about his son's success in the future. Thief also said sorry to them and said that he was hungry so was looking for something to eat. Four friends gave the thief lots of food and said him not to do the theft again.

They all returned to their home with sweet memories of future.

THE ADVENTURE IN THE FROSTBITE CAVES

One day four friends were playing Cricket. There were two teams. Captains of the two teams were Joseph and Ryder respectively. Joseph's team was batting first and the captain was on the strike. He hit the ball hard up in the sky and it goes all the way in the sky out of the ground and it was a huge six!!

Ryder goes to find the ball outside the ground. He found the ball & picked it up. He saw something on the ground. It was like a box in the ground. He tried to pull it from the ground, but it didn't came out. He shouted and called his friends to tell them what he had seen. Hey friends – "I found something here on the ground". They all tried to pull it from the ground but it was stuck deep in the ground. They dig the mud to pull the box out from the ground.

They managed to pull the box. Jack opened the box. As the box opened, a door opened in the tree as well. They all were astonished to see the door in the tree. There was a map in the box. They looked at each other in wonder!!

It looked like a treasure map. They decided to open the gate and enter into the tree.

Jack opened the door and they all slowly entered into the gate. Inside the gate they saw a new world. There was a road in front of them. Across the road there was snow mountains.

Mary – "Wow, It's so beautiful!!!"

As they moved forward across the road and moved near the snow mountain, they saw a cave in the snow.

Joseph said – "Let's open the map and see

 What does it show?"

Mary- "It's showing Snow Mountain as well!! Let's go what we are waiting for?"

Ryder – "This seems to be Frostbite Cave!! Let's see, what is inside"

Finally they all moved towards the mountains and near the Frostbite cave.

"It's very dark in the cave" – said Mary

"Jack You only tell something, you are the most intelligent among all of us. Take us out of this trouble" – said Mary

"Yes, I have an idea. We can rub two stones and it can produce fire but we also need something which can catch fire and can hold the fire for some time – like a wooden fire torch" – Said Jack

"We need some dry woods and some dry grass or leave which can catch the fire easily"- Said Joseph

"Ok – let's find out dry grass, dry wood and some stones" – said Mary

They all gathered required things from nearby. After couple of

hours, they managed to make fire and make small wooden fire torch.

They all entered in the cave with the fire torch. They moved inside the cave.

"Let's go, something is coming from the back" – said Mary

"It's a big ball – Run! Run! Run!" – shouted Ryder

In front of them, there were two ways.

"There are two ways to go. Let's divide in two groups – one in left side and one in right side" – said Joseph

One side Jack and Ryder went by and other side Joseph and Mary went by"

In the right side – where Joseph and Mary were there – they found a box.

When Mary opened the box – she found small gold ball inside the box. It felt down and a word appears on the floor "Frosbite".

Then three words appeared on the floor one by one– "Road" -> "Oh my God" -> "Jiraffe"

Bit ahead from the passage there was a gate. There it was written to enter the password and it will get permanently locked after 5 wrong passwords.

Joseph tried – "Frostbite" – but no luck

They tried all three words one by one – but no luck

Joseph thought – we can try every word's first letter" It was Frog. It was their last chance and this time – as they tried, gate opened.

On the left – where Ryder and Jack went by – ball rolled towards them. They were running like a horse trying to escape from the big stone ball. But suddenly, a wall appeared in between the ball and Ryder and jack, which stopped the stone ball. They were re-lieved!!

As they moved ahead at some distance they met with Joseph and Mary. All friends were very happy to meet again!!

They all moved together – they found a room there and found lot of treasure there with gold, diamond & silver.

They picked up as much they could and stored it in their pockets. They went ahead – and found a gate in front of them.

On this gate – it was written that this gate will close forever in 1 second – once someone enter the gate.

So they could not go inside the gate.

Joseph said – "Let's hold our hands together and all of us moves in a single step in the gate"

Mary said – "let's practice before we actually enter the gate"

They practices few times so that they all move in together.

Finally they all stepped together inside the gate and just soon after they crossed the gate, it closed.

Once they crossed the gate – they found another box.

In the box – there were eleven small boxes. In one box – Joseph found a small gem – all other were empty. They kept it with them.

They decided to halt there for some time – to take some rest – while Joseph went bit ahead.

As he moved forward, he came across one pit on the way.

It was not clearly visible – how deep the hole was. So he threw a stone ball to listen the sound of stone and to know the depth of the hole.

He heard the instant voice of stone ball striking the earth. So, he understood that it was not a deep one.

Ryder- shouted "Is everything alright there?

Joseph – "No everything in not alright here. It is very dark here I cannot see much here."

He put his wooden fire torch down to see how wide the hole is. Now he could see that it is was not a big one and he could jump it.

So, he risked to jump it without much fear as it was not a very wide hole.

He moved forward after crossing this hole and after some time – he started seeing brightness coming from somewhere. He found a room there and some strange drawings were written on this:

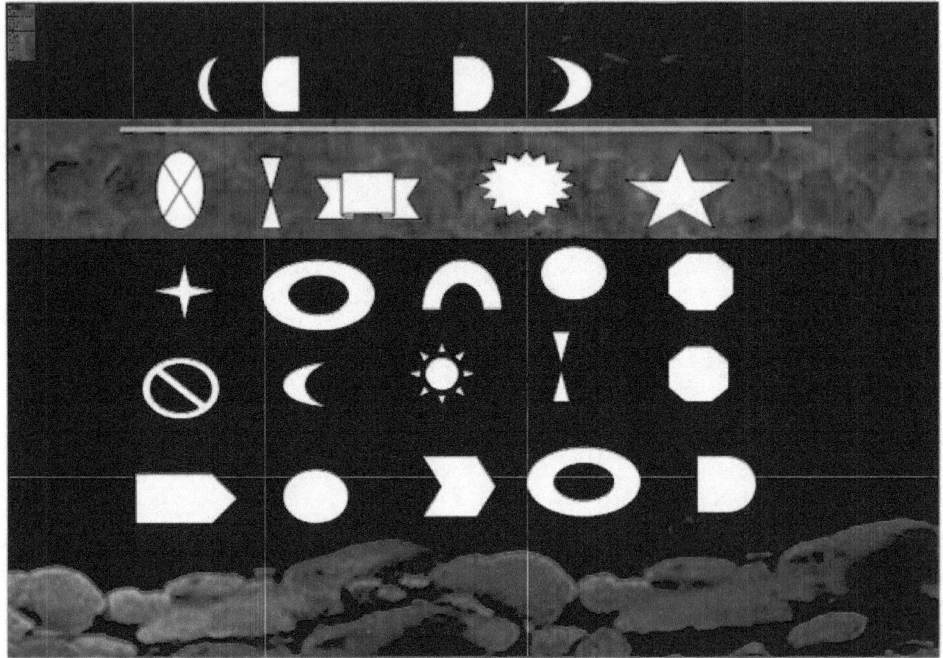

Joseph didn't know what to do. He saw the door had a lock with password. There were shapes on the lock. He thought for a while and could not find the answer. Oh it's moon's different shapes in the first picture. It should be a full moon.

He pressed the shape with full moon and the door opened slowly!!

He shouted in joy– "yes!!!!!!!!!!"

Ryder, Jack and Mary were still resting behind and they heard the voice of Joseph. Ryder was leaning on a wall – he found that he had pressed something by his back. Oh it was a button – magic happened then they were surprised to find themselves with Joseph near the room.

Joseph again shouted – when did you came here!!!

We don't know – Mary shouted!!

Jack and Ryder nodded their heads in surprise.

After moments of wonder – they walked together in the room. In the room – it was written "Last Room".

They also found one big key and one big lock in the room.

Jack inserted the key in the lock. A door opened and they found the way outside to the cave. Now all of them were out of the cave.

They all were relieved to finally came out of the cave. They all smiled and felt safe.

There was a big house there. They knocked the door. One old man opened the door. Old man asked – "From where are you guys coming?"

Jack replied – "We are coming from Frostbite caves."

Old man laughed and said – "You must be joking. No one ever came back from those caves"

The children looked at each other in wonder. Jack said – "We are coming from caves only."

Old man said – "Then you guys must be very brave and intelligent. Let me know – brave kids – how can I help you."

Jack said – "if you can help us to go to our playground– it will be great!!

Old man said – "Yes of-course. Please come with me."

Old man walked with them and took them to the magical tree.

Children thanked him and said good-bye.

They were again in their playground. They played and left for their home with wonderful memories.

To be Continued in the next part…..

Author: Ishant Aggarwal

CAR REPAIR
FAST FOOD